CHARLEY HARPER'S

WHAT'S
in the
WOODS?

A Nature Discovery Book

Text by Zoe Burke

Pomegranate **kids**®
AGES 3 to 103!

Published by PomegranateKids®, an imprint of
Pomegranate Communications, Inc.
19018 NE Portal Way, Portland, OR 97230
800 227 1428 | www.pomegranate.com

Pomegranate Europe Ltd.
Unit 1, Heathcote Business Centre, Hurlbutt Road
Warwick, Warwickshire CV34 6TD, UK
[+44] 0 1926 430111 | sales@pomeurope.co.uk

To learn about new releases and special offers from Pomegranate, please visit www.pomegranate.com
and sign up for our e-mail newsletter. For all other queries, see "Contact Us" on our home page.

This product is in compliance with the Consumer Product Safety Improvement Act of 2008 (CPSIA). A General
Conformity Certificate concerning Pomegranate's compliance with the CPSIA is available on our website at
www.pomegranate.com, or by request at 800 227 1428.

Library of Congress Cataloging-in-Publication Data

Burke, Zoe.
 Charley Harper's What's in the woods? : a nature discovery book / Zoe Burke.
    p. cm. — (A nature discovery book)
 Summary: Simple, rhyming text introduces individual woodland birds and animals as seen in Charley Harper's
illustration "Penitentiary Glen" ("Birducopia"), which is shown as a whole on a fold-out page at the end.
 ISBN 978-0-7649-6453-4 (hardcover)
 [1. Stories in rhyme. 2. Forest animals—Fiction. 3. Harper, Charley, 1922-2007—Fiction.] I. Harper, Charley,
1922-2007, ill. II. Title. III. Title: Charley Harper's what is in the woods? IV. Title: What's in the woods?
 PZ8.3.B95249Chl 2013
 [E]—dc23
                              2012037972

Pomegranate Catalog No. A216
Designed by Stephanie Odeh

Printed in China
22 21 20 19 18 17 16 15 14 13   10 9 8 7 6 5 4 3 2 1

LET'S go walking through the woods—

There'll be so much to see!

Can you guess what's up ahead?

Come along and walk with me.

FIRST, let's start by looking up

Into the cloudless sky.

There's the tail of a startled Grouse!

Look! A Swallowtail Butterfly!

OTHER birds sit in the trees;

They're looking right at you.

The Scarlet Tanager sure is red!

The Blue Jay is so blue!

WHOSE songs are those? Listen, now—
A Cardinal! Can you hear?
It sounds as though he's having fun;
He sings to us, "Cheer, cheer!"

AND over there, a Wood Thrush sings

His flutelike song so well,

Accompanying the Water Thrush,

Whose voice rings like a bell.

WHAT a lovely melody

The little Warbler sings!

And now a "Hoot!" from watchful Owl—

His eyes are round as rings!

WHAT'S that sound from over there,

That fast, repeating beat?

A Red-Bellied Woodpecker pecks a tree,

Hoping for a treat.

A Pileated Woodpecker,

With crest so red and proud,

Joins the drumming with his beak.

His noise is twice as loud!

A rustling movement at our feet—
Can you identify
The bushy tail and showy stripes?
It's Chipmunk dashing by!

THE Squirrel is eyeing us in case
We find the nuts he's stashed.
Let's walk away and leave him be—
What's that? Something just splashed!

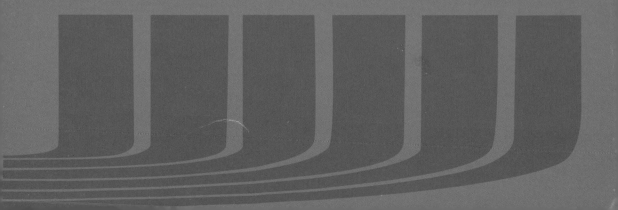

CROWS as black as black can be

Are cackling like they're talking.

And there's a Turkey to our left

Who gobbles while he's walking.

AHA!

A Wood Duck on the stream—

A graceful, pretty swimmer.

Now, as he flies on strong, broad wings,

His colored feathers shimmer.

LOOK closely now: upon the rock
A Salamander crawls.
And, oooh! Is that a Snake I see
Slithering by the falls?

SOMETHING black and white runs by—

A Skunk! Let's keep away.

If she's frightened, she'll let loose

Her not-so-fragrant spray!

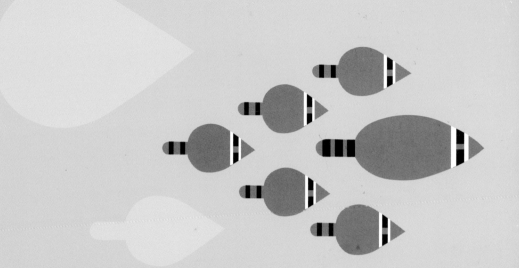

ACROSS the path some Raccoons amble,

Bellies round and low.

Their tails are striped, their faces masked;

They waddle as they go.

QUICK!

There's a 'Possum climbing up

That tall Striped Maple tree.

His tail is pink, and so's his nose.

Do you think he sees me?

AS we walk, be quiet now—
Don't scare the Fawn ahead.
Her eyes are wide, her ears alert.
She sees us—now she's fled.

AN eerie creature startles us,

Emerging from a hole.

His funny snout sniffs all about:

A curious Star-Nosed Mole!

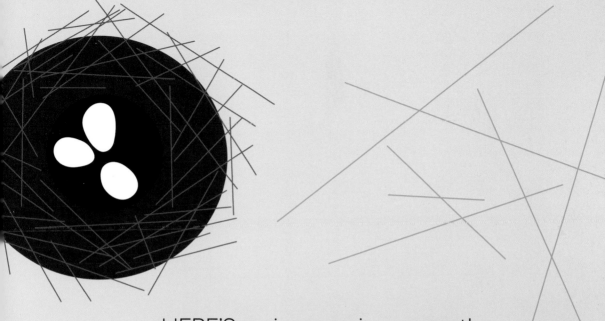

HERE'S a nice surprise—a nest!
Don't touch, but come and see—
Precious eggs, ready to hatch.
Let's count them: one, two, three.

THROUGH Ferns, Mayflowers, and Trilliums

Let's stroll and start a search

For a Jack-in-the-Pulpit . . . I spy one!

And there's a white-barked Birch.

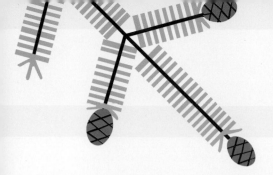

THE trees provide a canopy
And clean, refreshing air.
Beech and Hemlock all around—
Leaves rustle everywhere.

OUR walk is done; can you recall

The animals we met?

The birds and plants and leaves and trees?

You'll find them here, I'll bet!

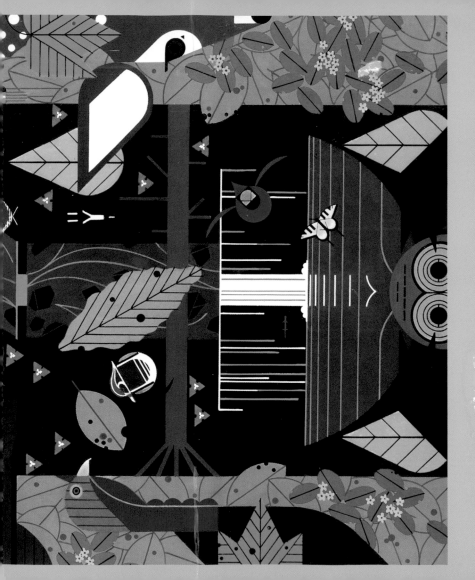

Charley Harper's **WHAT'S** in the **WOODS?**

KEY:

1.	Grouse	11.	Turkey	22.	Striped Maple
2.	Swallowtail Butterfly	12.	Red-Bellied Woodpecker	23.	Fawn
3.	Scarlet Tanager	13.	Pileated Woodpecker	24.	Star-Nosed Mole
4.	Blue Jay	14.	Chipmunk	25.	Nest
5.	Cardinal	15.	Squirrel	26.	Ferns
6.	Wood Thrush	16.	Wood Duck	27.	Mayflowers
7.	Water Thrush	17.	Salamander	28.	Trilliums
8.	Warbler	18.	Snake	29.	Jack-in-the-Pulpit
9.	Owl	19.	Skunk	30.	Birch
10.	Crows	20.	Raccoons	31.	Beech
		21.	Opossum	32.	Hemlock